CAPTAIN AWESOME
and the TRAPDOOR

By STAN KIRBY

Illustrated by GEORGE O'CONNOR

LITTLE SIMON

New York London Toronto Sydney New Delhi

LITTLE SIMON

An imprint of Simon & Schuster Children's Publishing Division • 1230 Avenue of the Americas, New York, New York 10020 • First Little Simon paperback edition March 2019 • Copyright © 2019 by Simon & Schuster, Inc. • All rights reserved, including the right of reproduction in whole or in part in any form. • LITTLE SIMON is a registered trademark of Simon & Schuster, Inc., and associated colophon is a trademark of Simon & Schuster, Inc. • For information about special discounts for bulk purchases, please contact Simon & Schuster Special Sales at 1-866-506-1949 or business@simonandschuster.com. • The Simon & Schuster Speakers Bureau can bring authors to your live event. For more information or to book an event contact the Simon & Schuster Speakers Bureau at 1-866-248-3049 or visit our website at www.simonspeakers.com. • Designed by Jay Colvin. • The text of this book was set in Little Simon Gazette. • Manufactured in the United States of America 0219 MTN
10 9 8 7 6 5 4 3 2 1
This book has been cataloged with the Library of Congress.
ISBN 978-1-5344-3315-1 (hc)
ISBN 978-1-5344-3314-4 (pbk)
ISBN 978-1-5344-3316-8 (eBook)

Table of Contents

SD

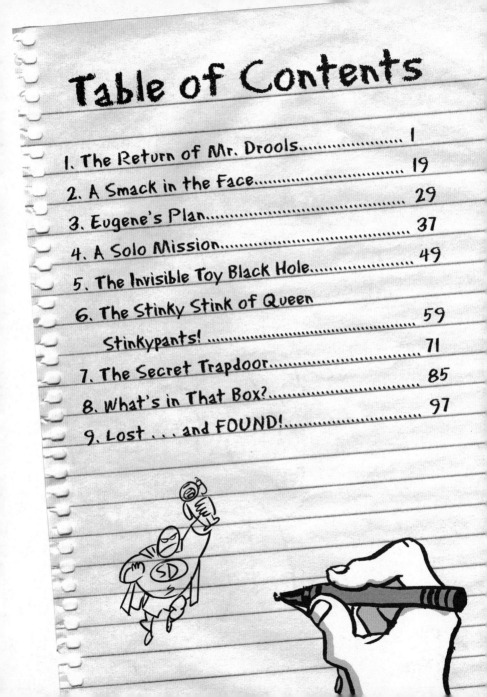

CHAPTER 1

The Return of Mr. Drools

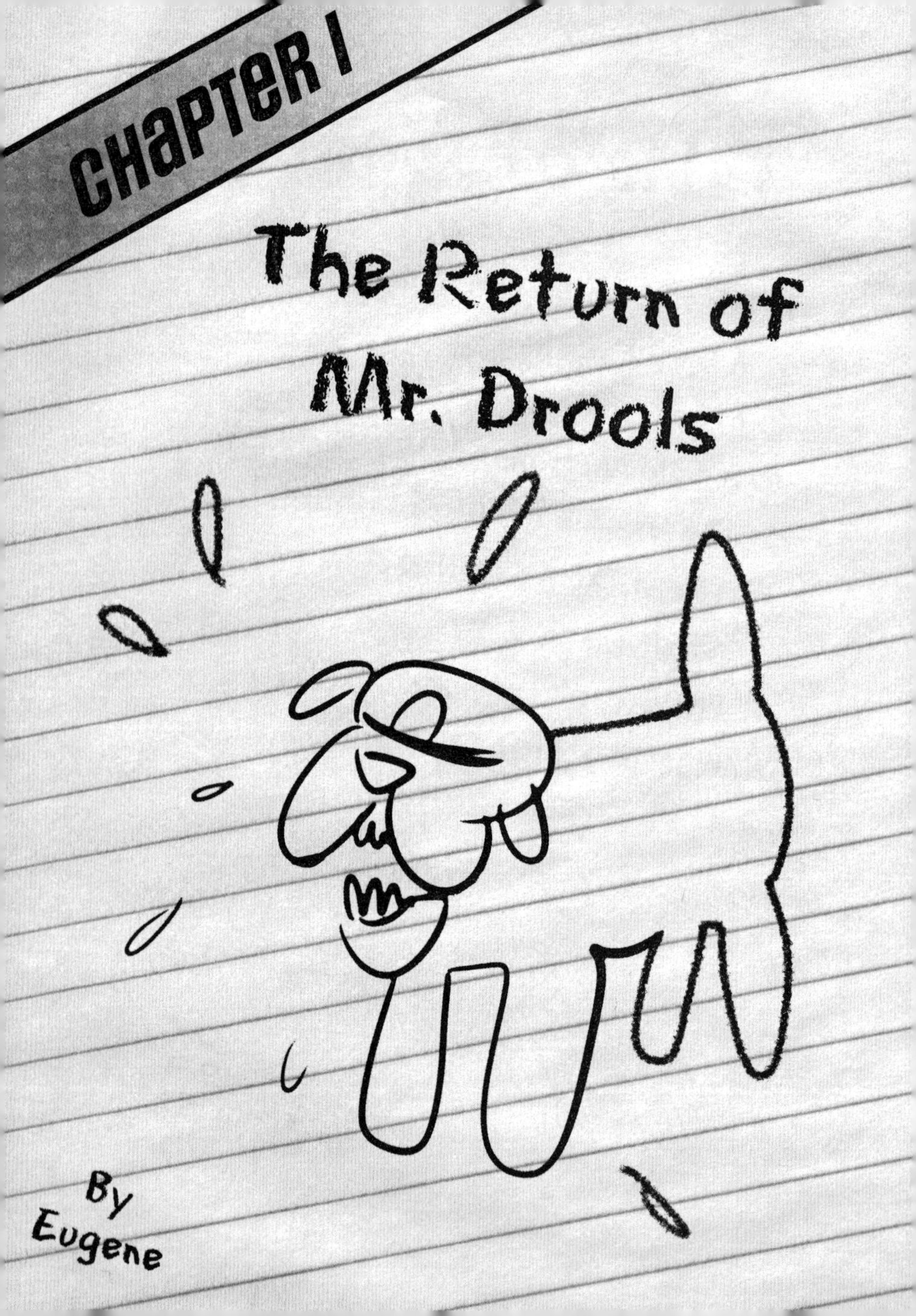

By Eugene

Behold! The time for Sunny- view Superhero Squad supersnacks is at hand!" Eugene McGillicudy called out.

That meant it was snack time.

Eugene, Charlie Thomas Jones, and Sally Williams had gathered in Eugene's tree house, aka the top secret clubhouse of the Sunnyview Superhero Squad.

"On the count of three, let's

reveal our supersnacks," Eugene instructed. "One, two, three!"

"I've got packets of green stuff," Charlie said. "It's either green tea or alien space goop."

"I have a box of sugar-free, gluten-free cookies," Sally said.

Eugene held up a plastic container and popped off the

lid. "I have . . . leftover lasagna! I declare that we make a tasty snack out of these," he said. "And we'll invent our own Superhero Squad Combo Meal!"

The trio of heroes combined their snacks at the Table of Justice. Eugene's lasagna formed the bottom layer.

"Cookie crumbles!" Sally crumbled the gluten-free cookies on top.

"Teatime!" Charlie opened two packets of tea and shook the green flakes over the cookies. "It's so colorful!"

"Bite time!" Eugene said, and he pulled a fork from his backpack.

BARK!
GROWL!
SNARL!

"Wh-what is that?" Charlie asked.

"Beast noises!" Sally said. "It can only be . . . Mr. Drools!"

Mr. Drools was the drooly dog-beast from the Howling Paw Nebula.

The Sunnyview Superhero Squad had defeated him before, but it seemed he was back.

"This is a job for the Sunny-view Superhero Squad!" Eugene declared.

BACKPACK!
UNZIP!
SUPERHERO!

Within minutes Captain Awesome, Super-sonic Sal, and Nacho Cheese Man were ready for action. "To the ladder!" Captain Awesome cried.

"My cheese is ready!" Nacho
Cheese Man yelled, holding two
cans of spray cheese. "Jalapeño
Cheddar and Garlic Swiss are fully
loaded."

"He's close," Captain Awesome
said as he climbed down the ladder.

"I can smell his stinky breath from here."

Before the superheroes could say anything else, Mr. Drools appeared.

"There he is!" Supersonic Sal cried. "Hey, what's in his mouth?"

Mr. Drools had something in between his ginormous drooling jaws, and his acid drool splattered on the grass.

"There's only one way to find

out," Nacho Cheese Man said. "We have to get him to drop it."

"We'll need our secret weapon," Captain Awesome said.

"One Hypersonic Mega Drool Treat coming up!" Supersonic Sal reached into the secret pocket of her supersuit and pulled out a dog treat.

She tossed the dog biscuit to Captain Awesome, but Mr. Drools jumped to snatch it out of the air.

"I'm on it!" Nacho Cheese Man yelled. He blasted the dog treat with a spray of Jalapeño Cheddar, which knocked it away from the snapping jaws of Mr. Drools and into Captain Awesome's waiting hand.

Captain Awesome caught the dog treat and rolled it in front of Mr. Drools. The drooling beast's eyes widened. He dropped what was in his mouth, grabbed the treat, and happily ran back to his *bark*yard.

Supersonic Sal raced over to grab what Mr. Drools had dropped. Then the trio ran back to their clubhouse.

"Mission accomplished!" Nacho

Cheese Man exclaimed. "So what do we have here?"

Supersonic Sal opened her hand, and Captain Awesome smiled his biggest smile.

"It's Bunky Buddy!" he cried.

"The action figure that's all talk and no action?" Nacho Cheese Man asked. "I remember him!"

"Before I discovered Super Dude,

the greatest superhero in the known universe," Captain Awesome said, "I was a big fan of Bunky Buddy."

What's that you say? You've never heard of Super Dude? Super Dude is only the greatest superhero to ever appear in comic books. He's the whole *reason* Eugene, Charlie, and Sally became superheroes and started the Sunnyview Superhero Squad. But now back to Bunky Buddy.

Captain Awesome hugged the toy. "I missed you, Bunky Buddy! I was wondering what happened to you. I never knew you were trapped in the Howling Paw Nebula with Mr. Drools."

"I love a happy ending," said Super-sonic Sal.

"Now let's get out of here before

Mr. Drools finishes his Hypersonic Mega Drool Treat and comes back to drool up more chaos," Nacho Cheese Man said.

CHAPTER 2

A Smack in the Face

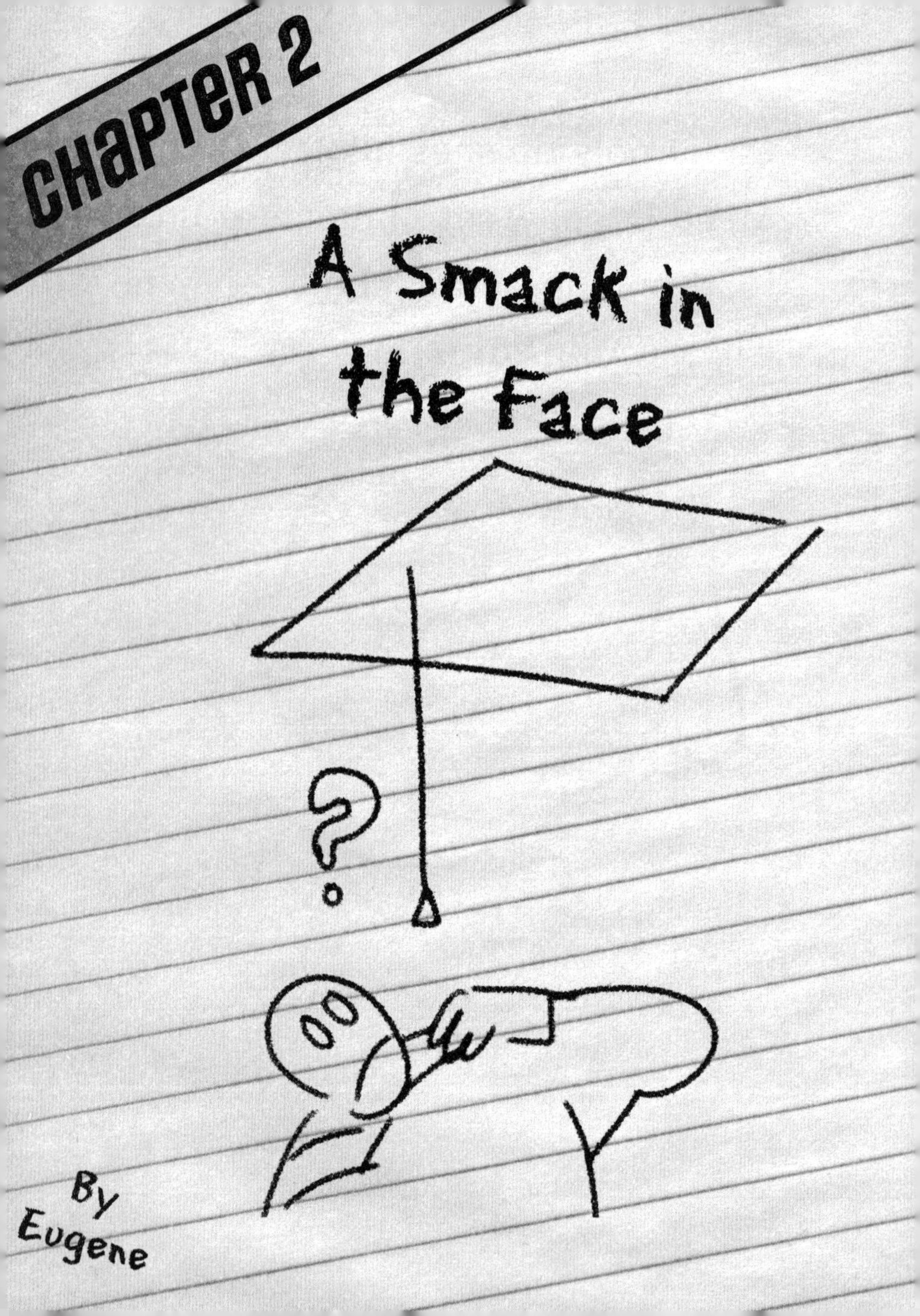

By
Eugene

Good morning! Are you ready to fight for goodness today?" Eugene's talking Super Dude Alarm Clock said the next morning. Eugene sat up in bed.

"You bet I am," he said to the clock. Eugene threw off his Super Dude blanket, removed his Super Dude pajamas, and dressed quickly.

"Let's go, Bunky Buddy!" he cried. Bunky Buddy was still in bed, lying on Eugene's Super Dude pillow. Eugene wasn't sure how long it had been since he'd played with Bunky Buddy—months? years?—and he didn't want to lose sight of him this time.

But being with Bunky Buddy now reminded Eugene of something. There were a *lot* of old toys Eugene hadn't seen in a while. Where was that robotic dog that barked anytime it sensed movement . . . which meant it barked nonstop? What about his Mighty Undies figurines?

I wonder where all of those old toys are, Eugene thought. Surely his mom would know.

He'd go ask her. "Let's go, Bunky Buddy!" he cried as he ran into the hallway.

Suddenly something hit him. Literally. Something hit him in the face.

Eugene looked up. A thin chain hung from the ceiling. It was swaying back and forth.

Well, that's a weird place to put a chain, Eugene thought. Then he looked closer. The chain was attached to the ceiling, but more specifically, it was attached to a *door* in the ceiling.

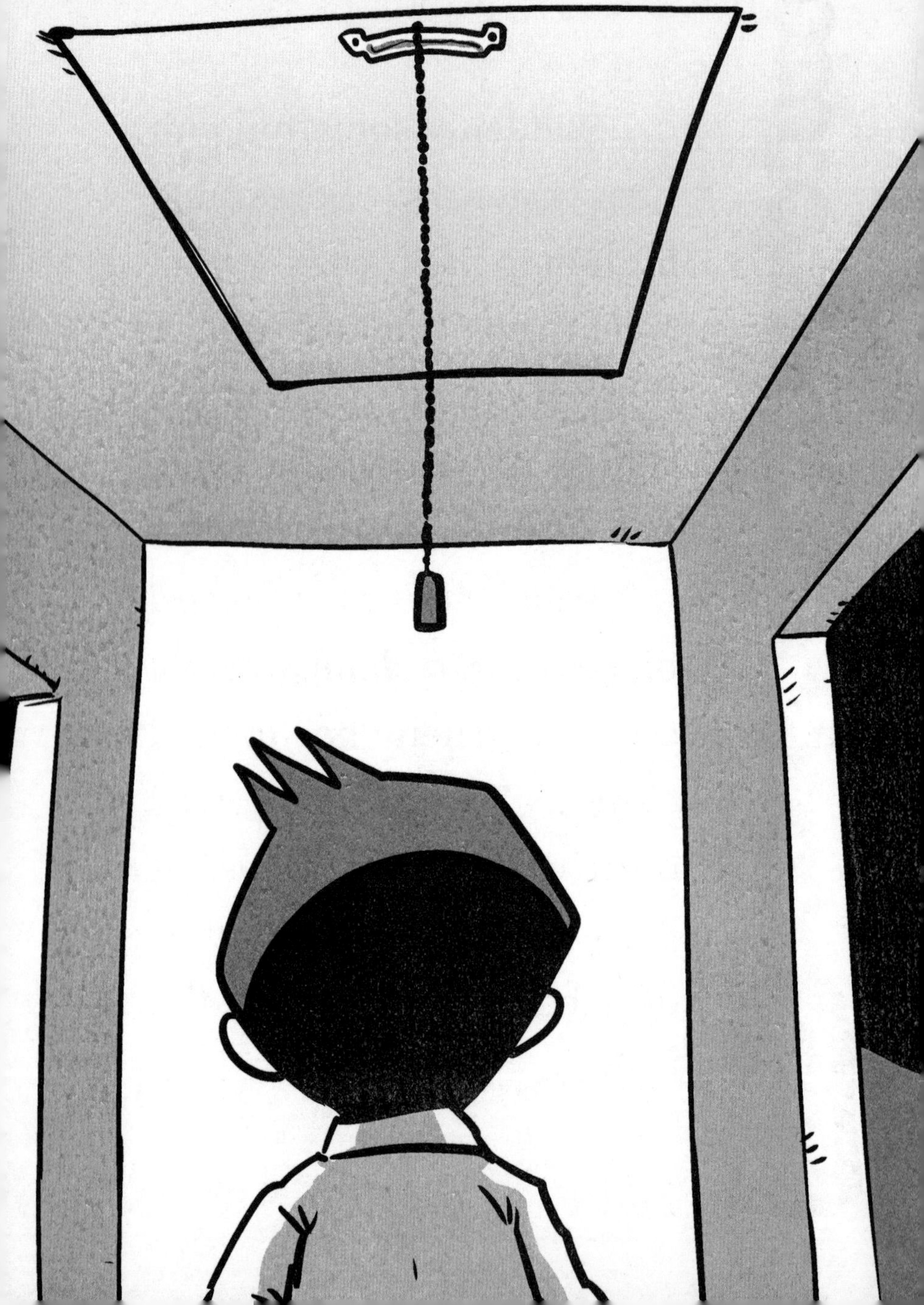

"Eugene!" his mom called from downstairs. "Breakfast!"

Eugene headed for the staircase, with Bunky Buddy clutched tightly in his hand. But he kept looking back at that door in the ceiling.

Finally Eugene walked downstairs and into the kitchen. "Hey, Mom—"

"Have a seat, Eugene!" Mrs. McGillicudy said. "Breakfast is just ready."

"Can I ask you a question?"

"Pancakes, Eugene," she replied.

"Don't let them get cold."

"I want to know about—"

"Syrup! Of course! It's already on the table," she said.

"Yes, but—"

"The butter's there too," she said. "So eat up before it's too cold."

The smell of the pancakes wafted into Eugene's nose, and he couldn't resist. He took a bite. Then another. Then another. His questions about where his old toys were and what that chain hanging from the hallway ceiling was would have to wait.

CHAPTER 3

Eugene's Plan

By
Eugene

No way," Charlie said. "There's a secret door at your house?" He bit into his cheese sandwich. "I wish I had a secret door at my house."

"How come you never noticed it before?" Sally asked.

Charlie, Eugene, and Sally were sitting at their usual lunch table in the cafeteria.

Eugene shook his head. "I guess I've just never looked up," he said.

"Maybe it's some kind of escape route," Sally said.

"In case monsters or aliens try to take over the world," Charlie added.

"Hmmm . . . it *could* be a trapdoor," Eugene suggested. "Maybe

my parents are waiting for some creature with thousands of eyes to fall through the roof so they can capture it!"

Eugene figured he'd find out what was on the other side of that

door eventually. But for now there was something even more important on his mind.

Eugene pulled Bunky Buddy from his backpack. "Thanks to the evil drooling creature from the Howling Paw Nebula, I found Bunky Buddy. But it got me thinking . . . where are all the other toys I used to play with?"

"Maybe the evil scientist Igor the Invisinator used his Invisi-blaster to turn them all invisible?" Charlie suggested.

"Or your dad accidentally threw them out?" Sally said.

Eugene gasped. "Threw them out?! No way. I'm going to look in my playroom when I get home from school today. If I don't find my toys, I'll call an emergency superhero meeting."

"Sounds like a plan!" Charlie said.

CHAPTER 4

A Solo Mission

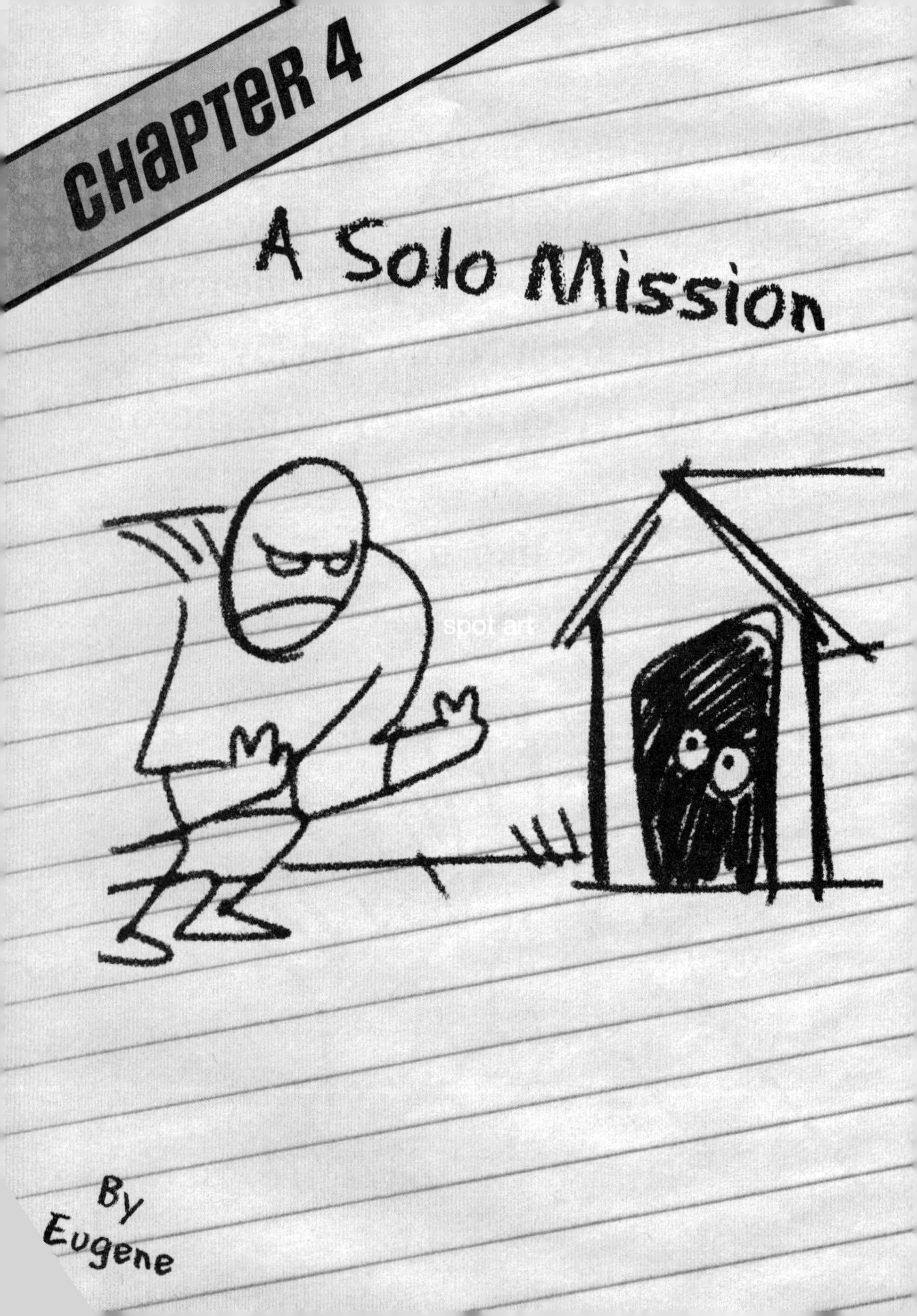

By Eugene

When Eugene got home from school that day, he raced upstairs to the playroom. He was excited to see his old toys again. "We're going to find them, Bunky Buddy, and have the best afternoon ever!" He held Bunky Buddy tightly in his hand. He wasn't going to lose him again.

Eugene looked around the play-room. *If I were an old toy, where would I hide?* He checked the cubbies, he dove into the closet, and he looked under the table. Nothing.

How can that be? he thought. *There's always something under the table!*

But there were no toys to be found. Where was Spuds the Cowboy Potato? Or Blockhead and his Blockmobile? Or Stuffy Rabbit?

They were gone! All gone.

Then Eugene had a thought. He

ran to his bedroom. He looked under his bed. Nothing.

He looked in the drawers of his dresser, and then under the dresser. He found two quarters, a nickel, and three orange jelly beans. He popped the jelly beans into his mouth. A little stale, but not too bad.

He looked in his closet, under his desk, and even in his laundry basket.

Eugene's old favorite toys weren't anywhere. Someone had taken them. But who?! And why?! And most importantly, where were they now?!

And then the answer hit him like a Triple Drool Slobber Attack. Where had he found Bunky Buddy in the first place?

In between the slobbering jaws of Mr. Drools. So if Mr. Drools had Bunky Buddy—did that mean Mr. Drools had *all* Eugene's toys? He needed to find out ASAP!

"Sorry, Bunky Buddy, but you have to stay here. I lost you once, and I can't risk losing you again,"

Eugene said, and he placed the toy high on a shelf, just to be safe.

Moments later Captain Awesome raced from Eugene's house toward the Howling Paw Nebula. The solo mission into Mr. Drool's barkyard was dangerous, but Captain Awesome couldn't wait for Nacho Cheese Man and Supersonic Sal.

I need a chew toy diversion, Eugene thought, and he picked up a squeaky ball from behind Mr. Drools's Drooly Doghouse.

SQUEAK! SQUEAK!

Captain Awesome squeezed the ball to get the pawed villain's attention, then threw it to the other side of the barkyard. And the plan worked! Mr. Drools ran out from his Drooly Doghouse in pursuit.

43

"Time to get my toys back!" Captain Awesome declared. He dove into the doghouse.

GASP!
SHOCK!
SURPRISE!

Other than chew toys, a stinky old bone, and what was probably a shoe at one time, the Drooly Doghouse was empty! There were no toys!

HOWWWWWLLLLL!

Uh-oh, thought Captain Awesome. *Have to escape! NOW!*

Captain Awesome scrambled from the Drooly Doghouse, and just in time. Mr. Drools was clomping back toward his doghouse.

That's the last time I go to the barkyard alone and risk getting droolified! Captain Awesome thought. *But if Mr. Drools doesn't have my toys . . . then who does?!*

CHAPTER 5

The Invisible Toy Black Hole

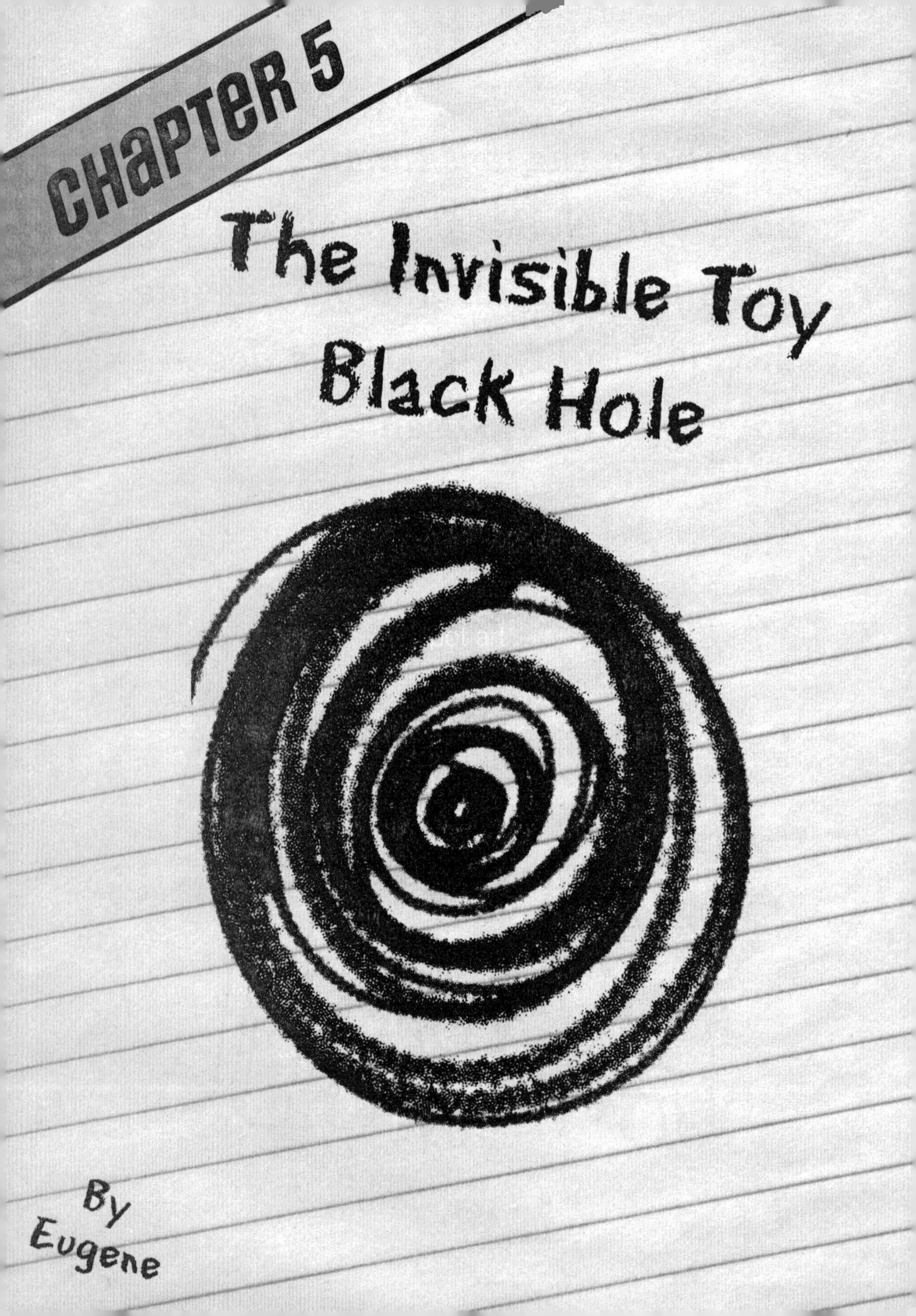

By Eugene

Minutes after his narrow escape from Mr. Drools, Captain Awesome stood in the middle of his living room with Charlie and Sally. "I've solved the mystery of my missing toys!" he declared.

"Did Santa Clones—the evil twin of Santa Claus who *takes* presents from good kids and gives them to naughty kids—swipe them from you?!" Charlie asked.

"I thought about that, Charlie, but Santa Clones always leaves his Stinky Stockings hanging on the fireplace when he leaves," Captain Awesome replied.

"And the only smelly socks in this house are mine. Since Mr. Drools didn't take them either, there can only be one answer: My toys were sucked into an Invisible Toy Black Hole by Tantrum Kid because all *his* toys were taken away during an Infinity Time-Out."

"An Invisible Toy Black Hole?!"

Sally gasped. "I don't want to be sucked into a different dimension! I have math homework to do tonight!"

"Don't worry," Captain Awesome said. "Invisible Toy Black  Holes only suck in toys. We just have to find it so I can get my stuff back."

"Then we should split up and search," Charlie suggested. "I'll look in the fridge—I mean, kitchen!"

"Sally, you take the living room. I'll check Molly's room," Captain Awesome said.

"Don't do it, Eugene!" Charlie cried. "You'll never get back out!"

Captain Awesome knew why Charlie was worried. It was because his little sister, Molly, was also none other than the evil

Queen Stinkypants, and her room was her secret lair.

"It's a chance I have to take," Captain Awesome said to Charlie. "If my sacrifice can save just *one* toy from Tantrum Kid, then it will be worth it! Besides, my Level-Twelve Anti-Stink Armor will protect me."

Captain Awesome pulled out a pair of rubber gloves that his parents used to clean the

bathrooms and snapped on a snorkel and diving mask that he'd gotten from . . . Wait, where *did* he get those things?

"Mo may, meam. Mets met mis mone mand mind mah mimisible mack mole!" Captain Awesome said with the snorkel in his mouth.

"Did you understand any of that?" Charlie asked as Captain

Awesome raced up the stairs toward his sister's bedroom.

"No. I forgot my Level-Twelve Anti-Stink Armor Translator at home," Sally said with a sigh.

As Captain Awesome bounded up the stairs, he was reminded of Super Dude No. 26, when Super Dude fought the Stink Bug and her army of Gashoppers. Super Dude teamed up with Daffo-Jill, and she used her Flower Power to throw them all in Perfume Prison.

"There's nothing better than the sweet smell of justice!" Super Dude said as he slammed the vanilla-scented prison door.

Captain Awesome didn't have any Flower Power, so he had been doing nose exercises, training for the day he'd have to go inside Queen Stinkypants's lair. But he knew no matter how many smelly socks he sniffed when he trained, it would never prepare him for the terrible stink of a . . .

DOUBLE DIAPER ATTACK!

Sorry, nose, but sometimes being a hero can really stink, Captain Awesome thought as he grabbed the doorknob and prepared for the worst.

CHAPTER 6

The Stinky Stink of Queen Stinkypants!

By
Eugene

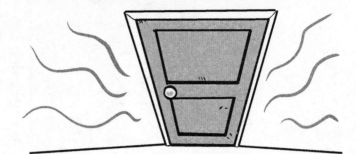

Captain Awesome opened the door and was instantly hit by the smell of poopy diapers! Even the Level-Twelve Anti-Stink Armor was no match for a Level-One-Hundred Double Diaper Attack. Captain Awesome tied a rope to his waist and looped the other end around the doorknob. If the smell made his legs too weak to walk, he'd still be able to pull himself from the room.

Where would a supervillain whose superpowers were all in her diaper hide my toys? Captain Awesome wondered.

And then he saw it!
LEGS!
ARMS!
SOMETHING THAT MIGHT BE A HELMET!

Captain Awesome took a deep breath and ran to a box across the room. The lid was open, and parts of toys were sticking out. Captain Awesome didn't have much time! Even his superlungs couldn't last forever.

Captain Awesome yanked the lid off the box, and his heart sank.

Instead of
seeing his
Rocket Rodent
action figure and
Newtundo Junior
Switcher game console,
he was greeted by a sparkly stuffed
panda, brightly colored plastic
horses, and a choo choo train with
a very big, smiling face.

*These are Queen Stinkypants's
toys!* he realized. *This must be a
fake-out!*

Captain Awesome wanted to
take a breath, but he knew he had

to get out of the room first!

Nose hairs . . . shriveling!

He stumbled toward the door.

Brain . . . melting!

Captain Awesome's
legs grew weak
from the smell.
He mustered
his last bit
of strength and
dove from the
room and into
the fresh air of
the hallway.

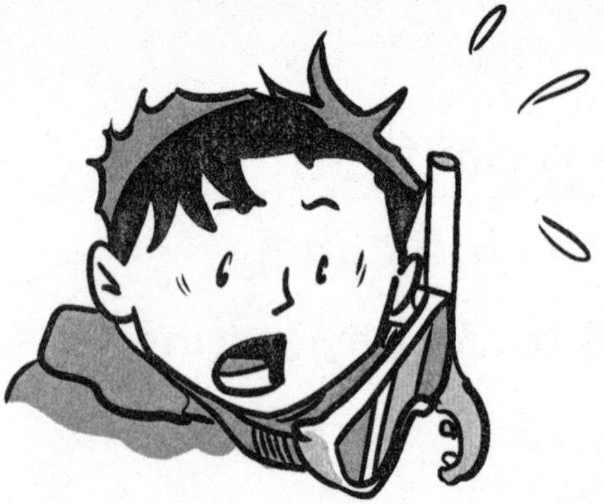

"Smell ya later!" Eugene said, and he slammed the bedroom door.

Eugene raced into the living room and saw Sally lying on the couch reading a book. Charlie stood

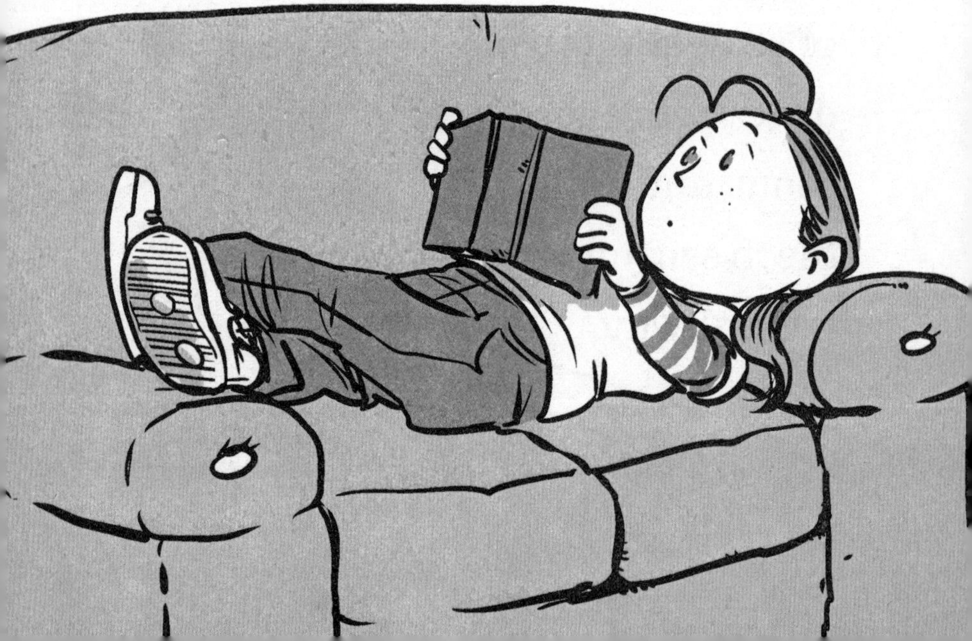

in front of the open fridge eating a slice of cheese.

"Guys! What are you doing?!" Eugene cried.

Sally leaped up and put her book down. Charlie closed the fridge door and spun around, like a kid caught with his hand in the cookie jar, except Charlie's hand was on a piece of cheese. He shoved the cheese into his mouth,

and he gave Eugene a smile.

"Sorry," Sally said. "But your parents have so many cool books, I guess I got a little distracted."

"And I didn't realize how hungry looking for Invisible Toy Black Holes would make me," Charlie confessed. "But you've gotta tell your parents to up their cheese game. They only have American cheese slices."

"Did you guys find anything?" Eugene asked.

"Nothing," Charlie replied. "Except the cheese slices. You?"

"Just Queen Stinkypants's baby toys," Eugene said. He sat on the couch next to Sally and shook his head. "We searched everywhere, and no Invisible Toy Black Holes." Eugene leaned his head back and looked up at the ceiling. The ceiling! The door in the upstairs hallway ceiling!

"Are you thinking what I'm thinking?" Sally asked Eugene with a smile.

"The secret trapdoor!" Eugene exclaimed.

"I don't want to go any place that has the words 'secret' and 'trap' in its name," Charlie said.

"*We* won't have to," Eugene said, "because the Sunnyview Superhero Squad will! Time to get MI-TEE!"

CHAPTER 7

The Secret Trapdoor

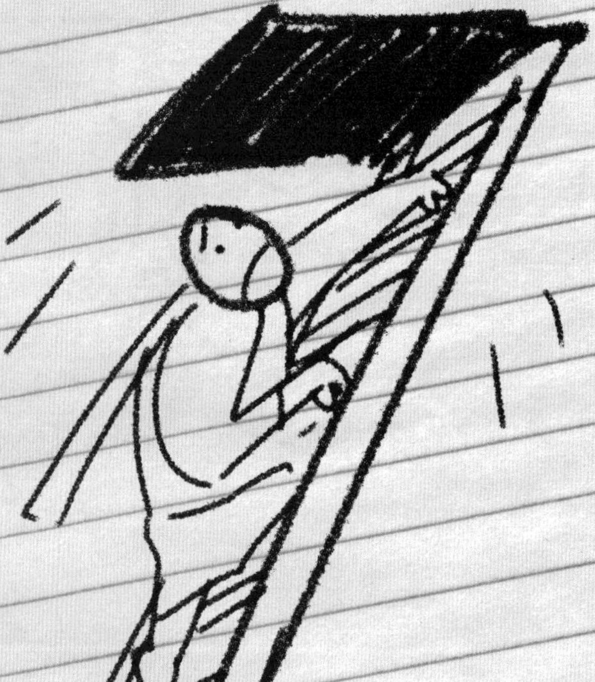

By
Eugene

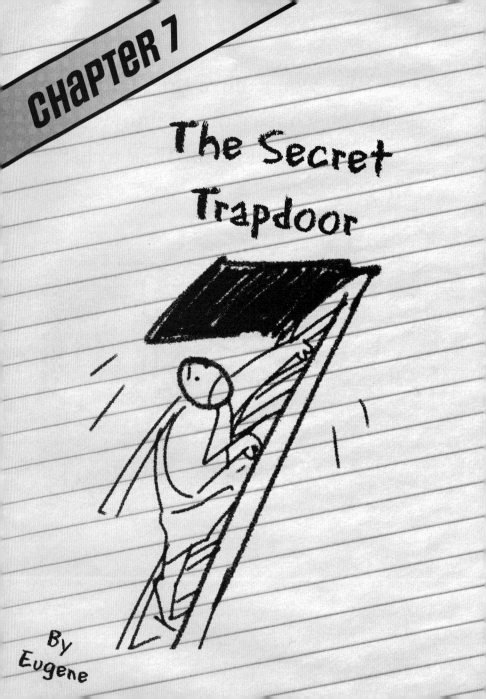

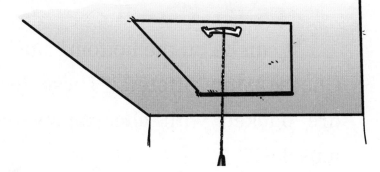

The kids changed into the world's greatest heroes who *weren't* Super Dude.

CAPTAIN AWESOME!
NACHO CHEESE MAN!
SUPERSONIC SAL!

"I'm not allowed to climb on any of the furniture," Captain Awesome said. "So we'll have to climb on each other's shoulders and make a Superhero Tower Stack."

"I can be on the bottom," Nacho Cheese Man offered. "These legs are packed with cheese-powered muscles!"

Captain Awesome started to lead the group toward the stairs, but then Supersonic Sal suddenly pulled them both back onto the couch.

"Look!" she whispered.

The three of them peeked over the top of the couch and saw the dynamic duo of difficulty!

PARENTS!
VEGETABLES!

Eugene's mom and dad were in the kitchen preparing dinner.

"Do you know what this means?" Captain Awesome sank back behind the couch.

"We have to give up our quest?" Nacho Cheese Man asked.

"No! It means I'm having peas *and* broccoli for dinner! Yuck! Who serves *two* kinds of vegetables?" Captain Awesome said. "Looks like we'll need to use all one hundred percent of our Super Sneak Tiptoe powers to get to the secret trapdoor. If my parents see Captain Awesome, they'll totally freak out and think I'm here because a giant two-headed octopus crawled up from the toilet and kidnapped their son."

"I *hate* when that happens." Nacho Cheese Man sighed.

The heroes wiggled their toes and stood up. But before they could tiptoe a single step, Eugene's mom looked over and said, "Is that you, Eugene?"

"Quick! Use your mind-erasing brain-wave blast!" Captain Awesome whispered to Nacho Cheese Man.

Before Nacho Cheese Man could fire off a brain wave, Eugene's  mom entered the living room. "Oh! Captain Awesome! I didn't know it was you. We meet again."

Captain Awesome leaped before his mom and struck a heroic pose. "Don't worry! Eugene was not kidnapped by a two-headed octopus that crawled up from the toilet! He's just, uh, studying many school things at his friend Charlie's, and that's why you won't find him in the house no matter how hard you look."

"Um, okay. Then I guess I won't

look for him," Eugene's mom said.
"So, to what do we owe this honor?
It's not every day we get real live
superheroes in our home. Is Miss
Pinky Head trying to, um, do pink

things to the world or something?"

"Her name's Little Miss Stinky Pinky, Mrs. McGillicudy," Supersonic Sal corrected.

Suddenly Captain Awesome's super-brainpower kicked up an awesome idea! "We're here because we need your help!" Captain Awesome declared. "There's a secret trapdoor that we need to investigate, but, um, well, I'm kinda not allowed to climb on the furniture, so . . ."

"You need my help opening it?" Eugene's mom asked.

"Pleeeeeeeeeeease!" the three

heroes said in unison.

Eugene's mom led the Sunny-view Superhero Squad to the trapdoor. She pulled the hanging cord to reveal . . .

A STAIRCASE!

"Be careful now," said Eugene's mom. "I'm not sure if that's just a trapdoor to our attic . . . or a gateway to the other side of the universe."

The three wide-eyed heroes peered into the darkness above them.

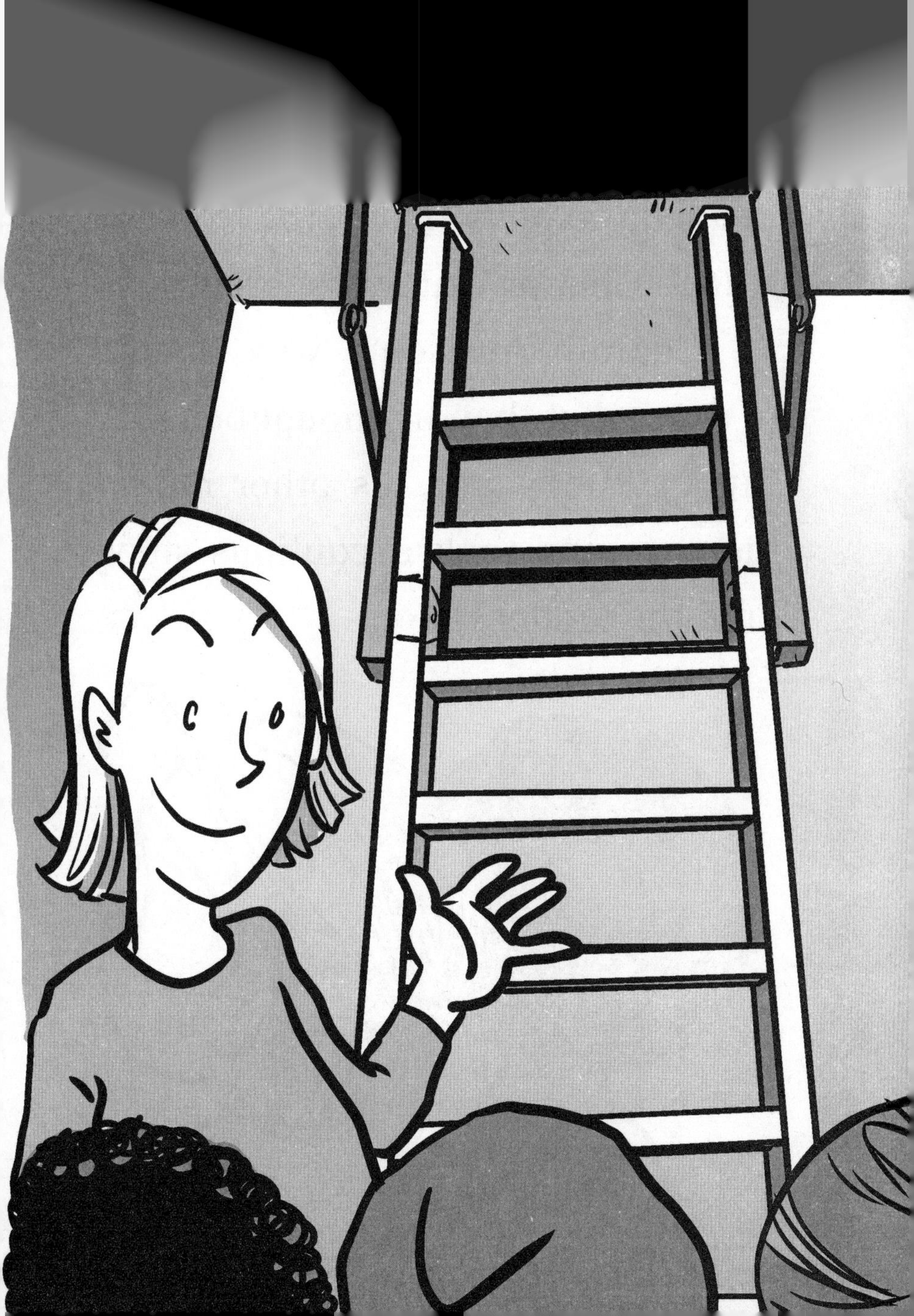

"I think I'd rather fight the two-headed octopus from the toilet," Nacho Cheese Man whispered.

Captain Awesome was about to agree, but then he thought about Bunky Buddy and his other missing toys and took a cautious step onto the ladder.

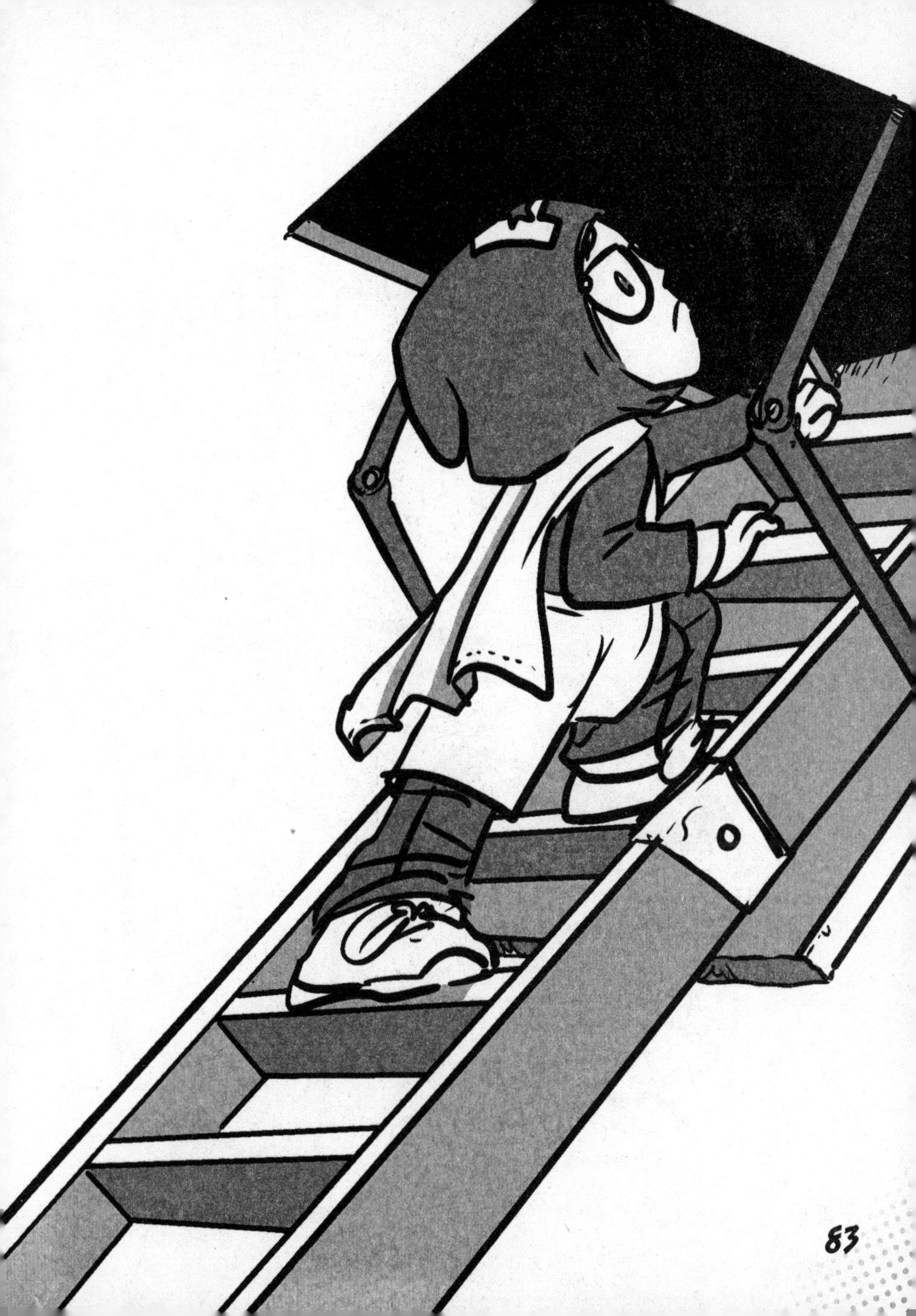

CHAPTER 8

What's in That Box?

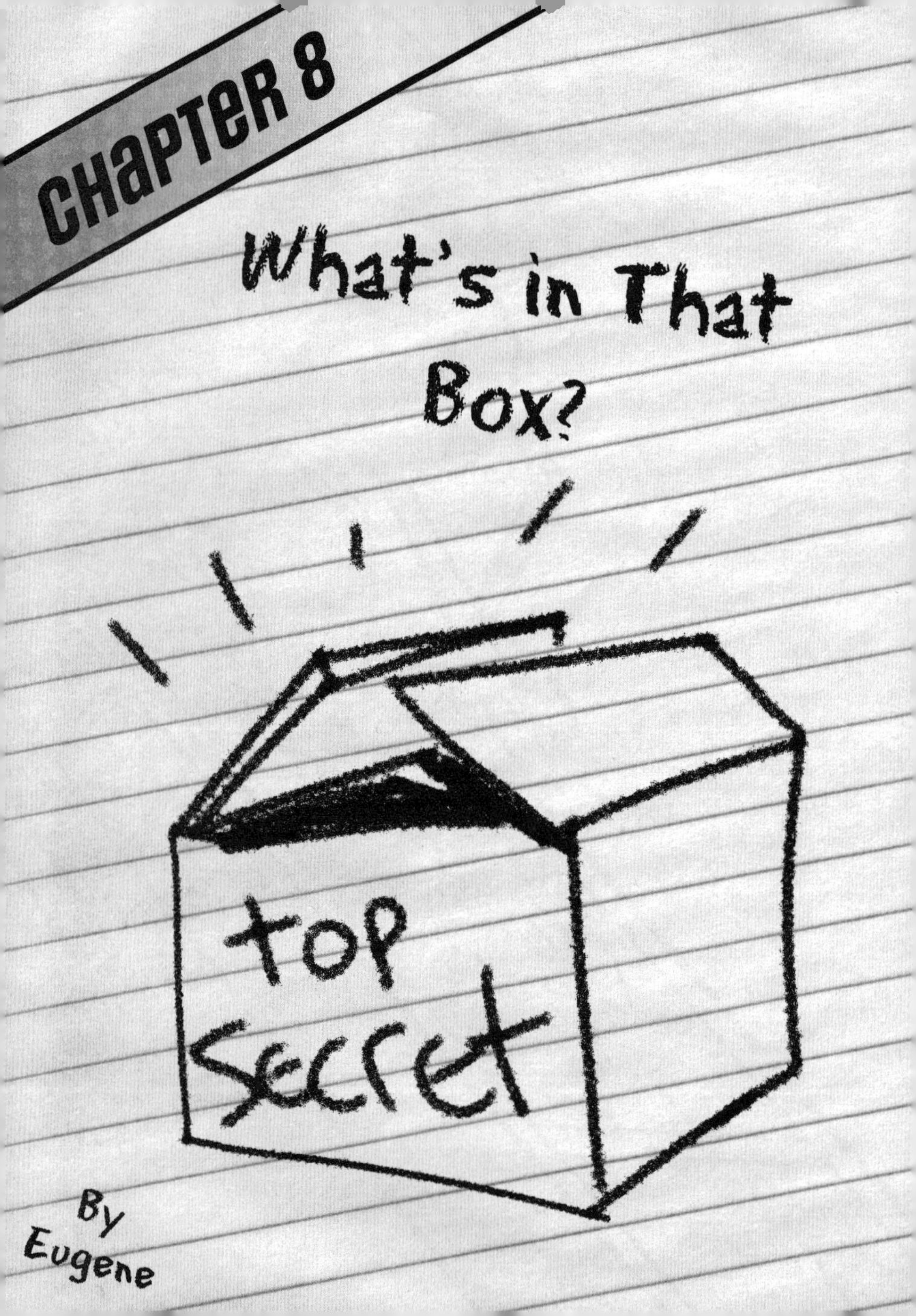
top secret

By Eugene

Captain Awesome led the Sunnyview Superhero Squad into the darkness.

He did his best to be brave, but he had a feeling this might be even worse than eating two types of vegetables for dinner.

"There's a light switch on the wall at the top of the stairs," Eugene's mom called up to them.

Captain Awesome, Supersonic

Sal, and Nacho Cheese Man lunged for the switch at the same time. A lone bulb flickered to life and created a dim overhead glow. Deep, dark shadows appeared on the walls.

"I don't think this is much better," Nacho Cheese Man said with a gulp.

"Remember what Super Dude said in number nineteen?" Captain Awesome asked.

"There can be light in the darkness . . . ," Supersonic Sal began.

"If you just have courage," Nacho Cheese Man finished.

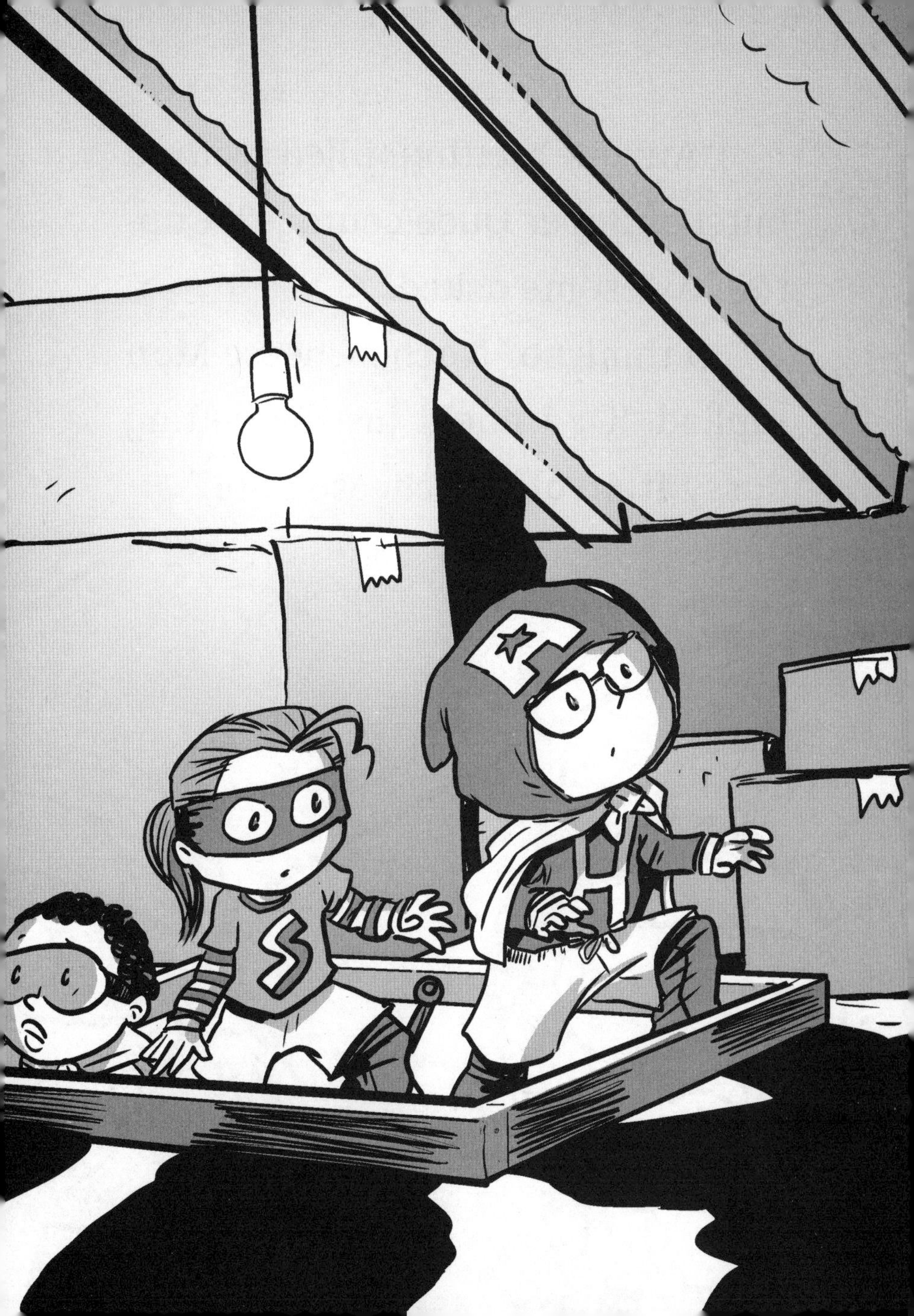

"Anyone getting filled with a burst of Super Dude courage?" Captain Awesome asked.

"I think so," Nacho Cheese Man replied. "Or I might just be getting gassy from all the cheese I ate."

Captain Awesome stepped further into the attic. Supersonic Sal and Nacho Cheese Man exchanged a nervous look, then followed.

As their eyes adjusted to the dim light, their fears suddenly faded away. What had looked like mysterious figures in the darkness were actually just . . . boxes! Stacks and stacks of boxes higher than any block tower Eugene had ever

made filled the attic. Some boxes looked new. Others looked old and dusty. Each box had a label.

Supersonic Sal pulled a small box from a stack. "It says 'Eugene's first haircut.' You don't think they kept the hair from your first haircut, do you?"

HATS

WEATERS

-MAS
ECORATIONS

HALLOWEEN
DECORATIONS

OLD
PHOTOS

TOWELS

Supersonic Sal opened the box. There wasn't any hair. . . . Just pictures of a one-year-old Eugene getting his haircut.

"You better hope those pictures never fall into Meredith Mooney's hands. Talk about giving a supervillain the ultimate weapon!" Nacho Cheese Man said with a laugh. He was clearly feeling better now!

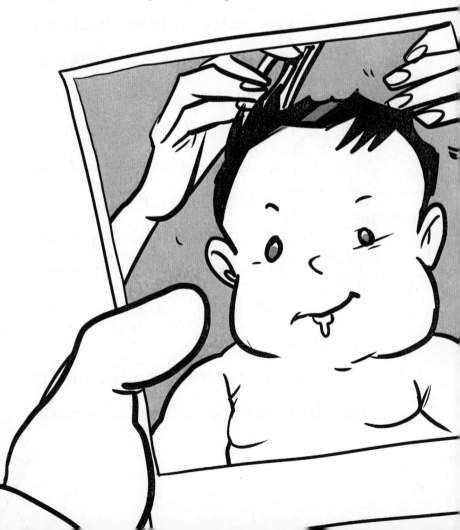

Captain Awesome scanned the boxes. One said WEDDING DRESS. Another was labeled EUGENE'S ART. There were boxes marked

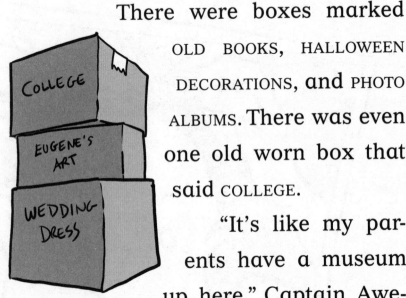

OLD BOOKS, HALLOWEEN DECORATIONS, and PHOTO ALBUMS. There was even one old worn box that said COLLEGE.

"It's like my parents have a museum up here," Captain Awesome said.

Captain Awesome pulled down a box labeled EUGENE'S BABY PHOTOS to make sure Supersonic Sal and Nacho Cheese Man wouldn't look through it. *Nothing worse than pictures of me as a drooling baby with food all over myself*, he thought.

But once Eugene had pulled down the box, it revealed a shocking surprise. . . .

A hidden box that said: TOP SECRET!

CHAPTER 9

Lost . . . and FOUND!

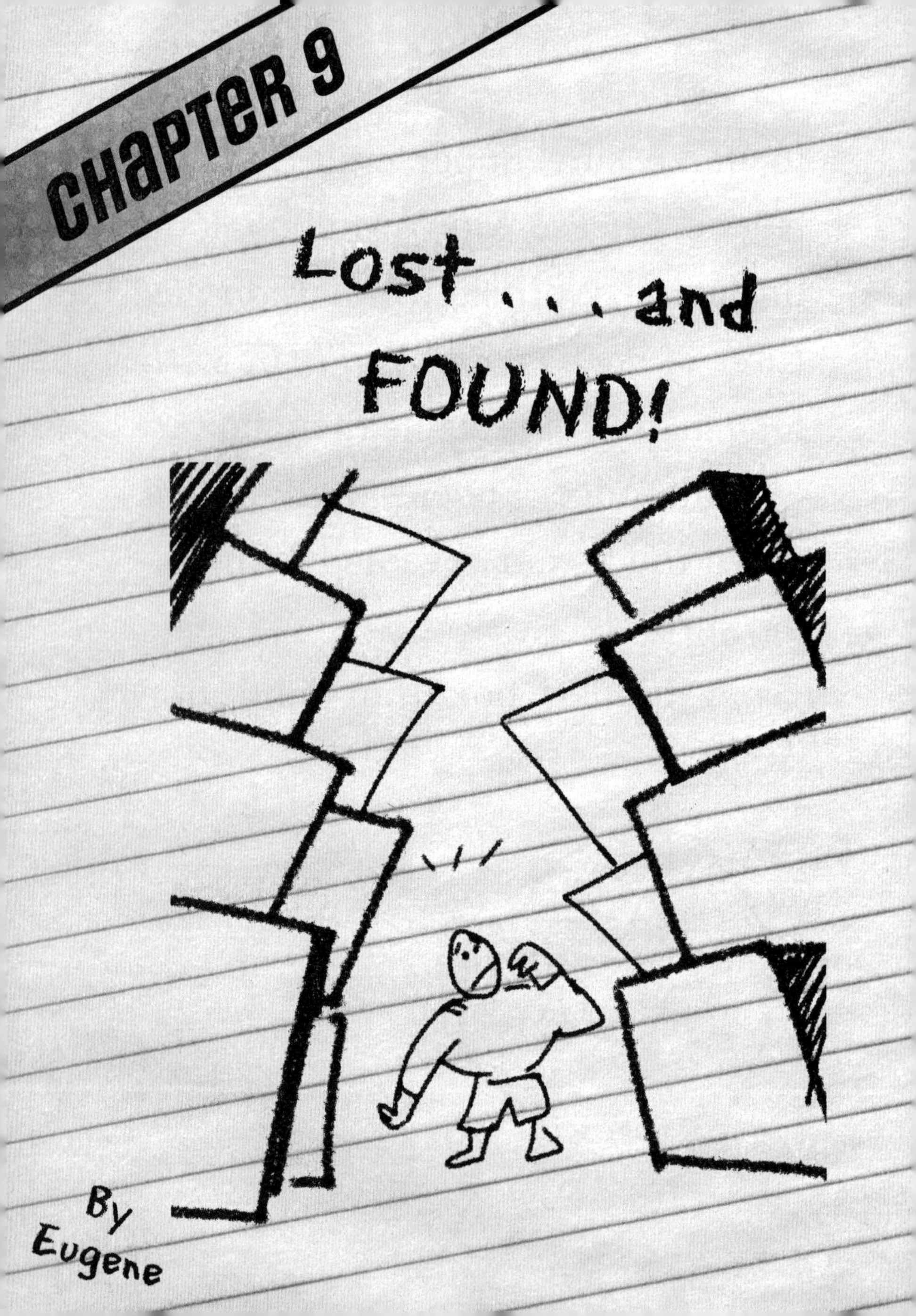

By Eugene

The three heroes stared at the mysterious box in silent awe, as if it were a giant dancing cookie.

"Should we open it?" Nacho Cheese Man asked.

"What if it's a trap? An actual trap. Not like this door that we thought was a trap," Supersonic Sal said.

"That's a risk I'm willing to take for my old toys," said Captain

Awesome. He slowly
reached out for the
lid of the top secret box, and just as
he was about to touch it, Nacho
Cheese Man yelled.

"By the hole in my Swiss cheese! Look!" he cried.

Eugene and Sally looked at where he was pointing. There, in the far corner of the attic was a box labeled . . .

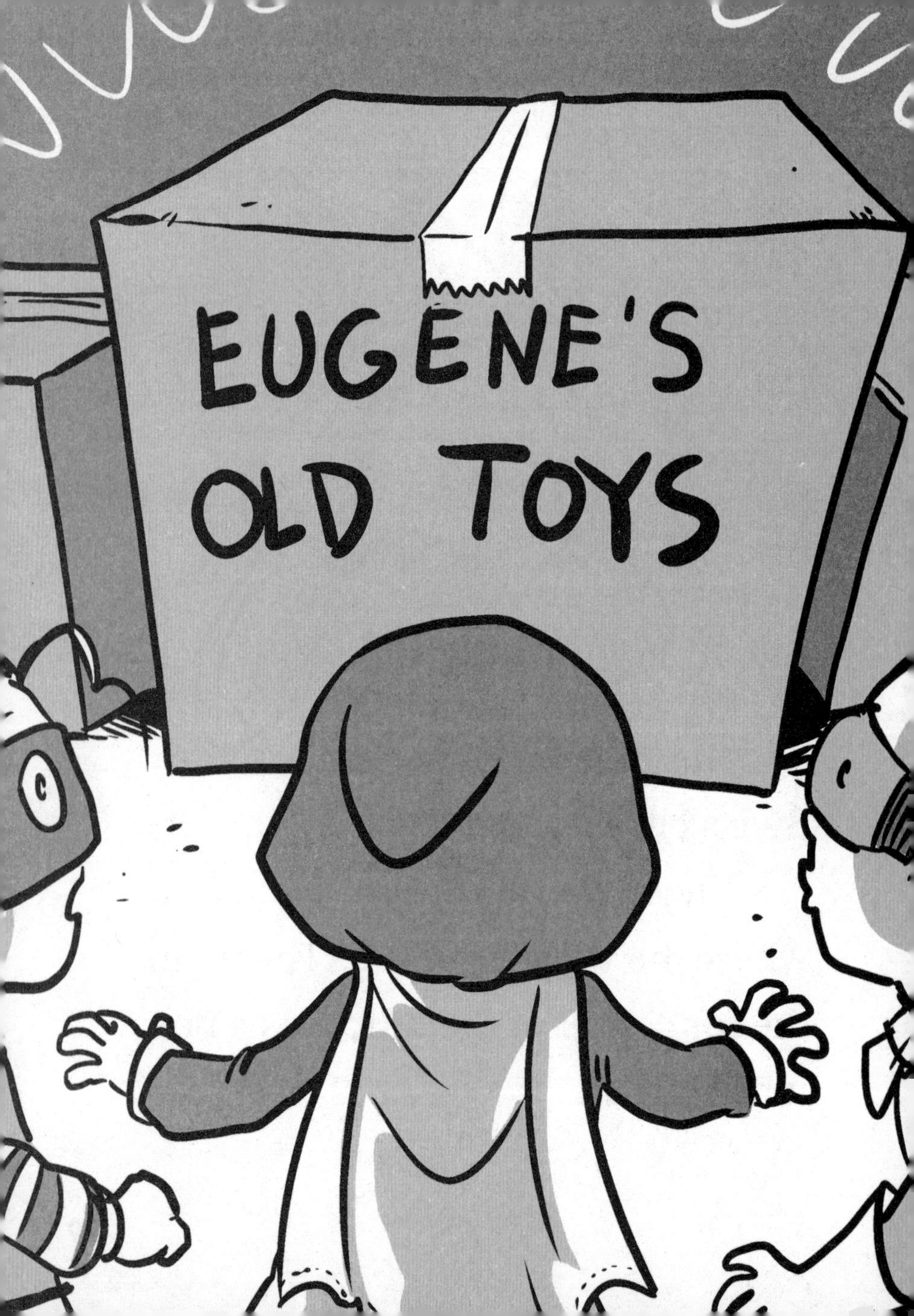
EUGENE'S
OLD TOYS

"EUGENE'S OLD TOYS!" they all said at once.

The trio ran to the box, hoping this was the end to their long and heroic search.

This was it. Captain Awesome slowly, carefully pulled up one side of the box top. Then the other. Inside were . . .

TOYS!

And not just *any* toys . . . EUGENE'S TOYS!

"Look! It's Arrrr2-D2 the robot pirate!" Captain Awesome pulled an old action figure from the box.

"And the Slime-osaurs from Dino Slime Island!" Supersonic Sal grabbed three gooey dinosaurs from the box. "It's Tricera-glops, Tyranno-slimeus Rex, and Ooze-odactyl!"

"And Don't Squeeze the Clown! That game always gave me the creeps," Nacho Cheese Man said.

They pulled toy after toy from the box. Spuds the Cowboy Potato! Blockhead and his Blockmobile! And even Stuffy Rabbit!

Captain Awesome
built a castle using the Blockhead
Building Blocks he found in the
box, and Supersonic Sal launched
an attack with Cowboy Battle Bots
and Cyborg Ninjas. Nacho Cheese

Man swooped in with a Super Dude Transmorpher Jet and saved the day, chasing the Cowboy Battle Bots and Cyborg Ninjas back into the box.

It may have been only a few minutes, or it could've

been hours. . . . The time slipped past without anyone paying much attention as they dug deeper and deeper into the box, pulling out one forgotten treasure after another.

After Supersonic Sal won the second game of Bees in My Cheese, Eugene's mom called

out from downstairs, "Captain Awesome? Any chance you know if
Eugene has come home yet? It's
time for dinner! Can you tell him
we're having pizza?" And then she
added in a quieter voice, "And peas
and broccoli."

"Okay, Mrs. McGillicudy, I'll

look for him," Captain Awesome called back. "But if I *do* find him, do you think his friends can eat dinner here too?"

"I'll text their parents now and ask, just in case they're already here with Eugene," Eugene's mom called back.

"We are!" said Nacho Cheese Man, excited to have pizza. "I mean, *they* are. Eugene's friends."

"What are we going to do with the toys?" Supersonic Sal asked.

Captain Awesome took a quiet moment to look at the memories

scattered on the ground before him.

"I think they should go back into the box," Captain Awesome answered. "I loved playing with them again, but the box says 'Eugene's *Old* Toys,' and the box is right. Most of them are from when I was in *first grade*. We can always

play with them if we want, but I think my parents' attic museum is the best place for them."

"That's very brave of you," said Supersonic Sal.

The heroes quickly put the toys back in the box and returned it to its place. Eugene felt good knowing that they'd always be up here, like old friends who'd have his back if he needed them to.

With everything once again in its place, the three heroes changed back into Eugene, Charlie, and

EUGENE'S
OLD TOYS

S

WINTER

Sally. Then they went downstairs and enjoyed an awesome pizza dinner that can only be described as . . .

MI-TEE!*

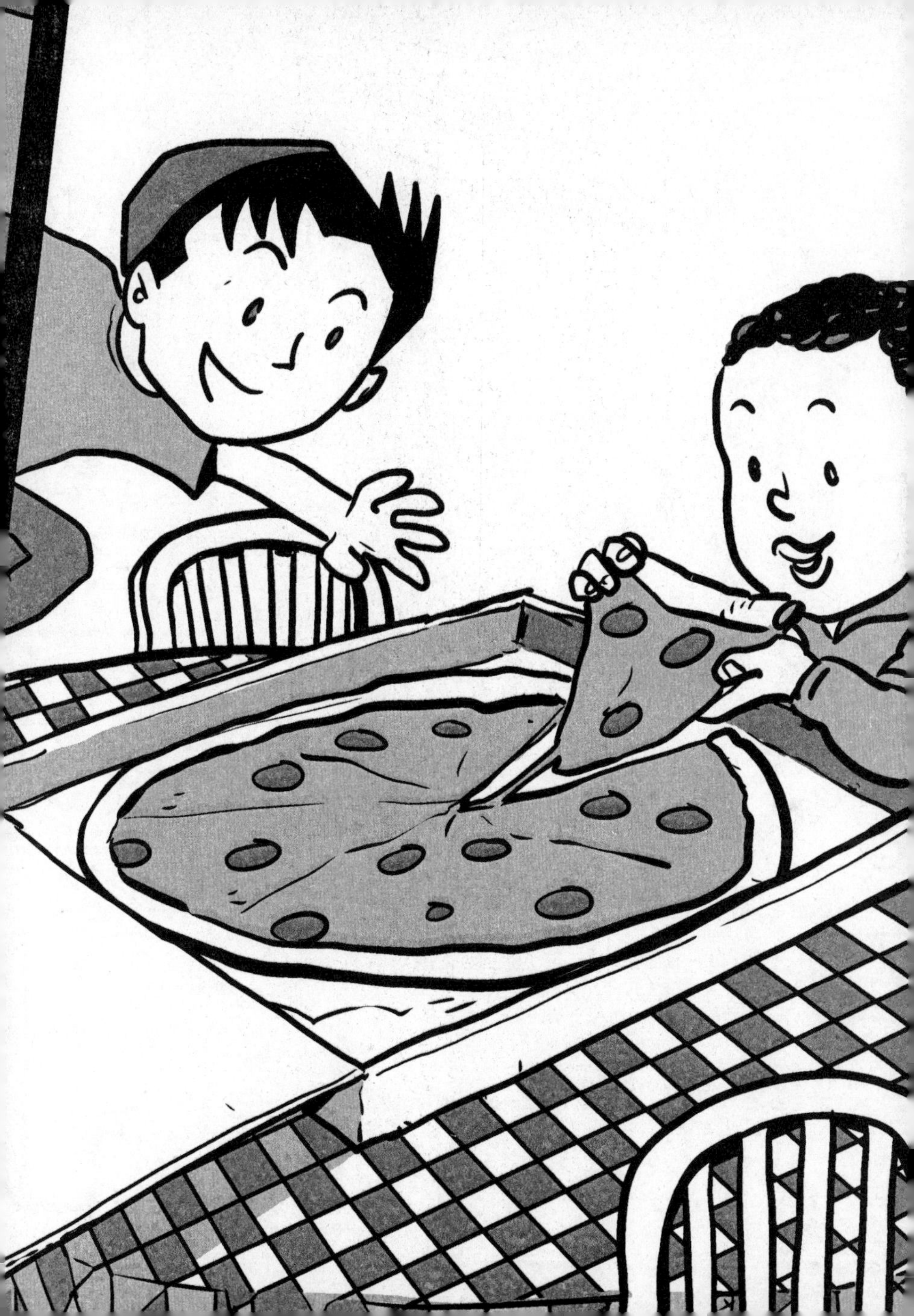

*In fact, it was so MI-TEE that they totally forgot about the top secret box they'd left behind in the

darkness of the attic. That would
have to wait for another day.

THE

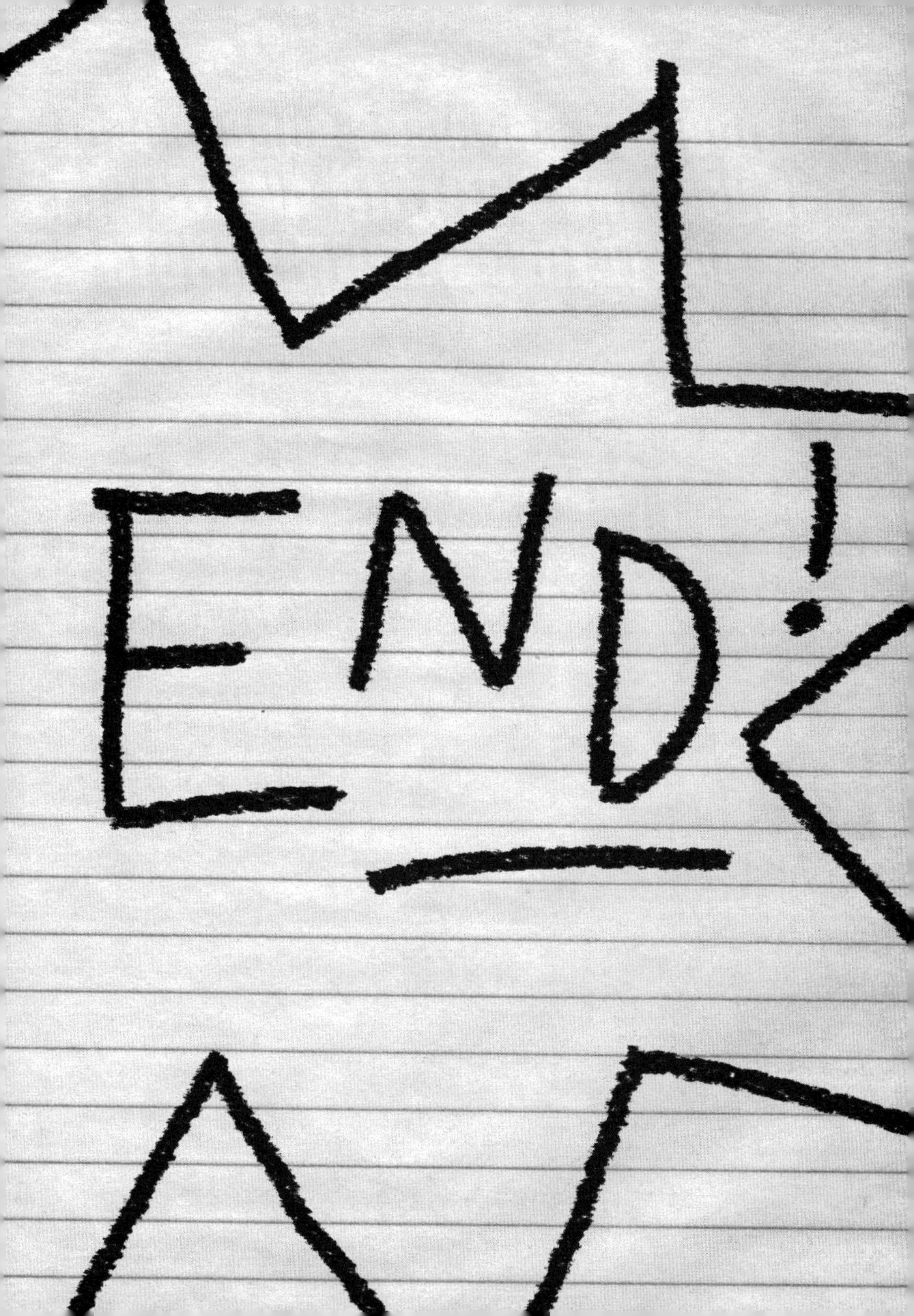
END!

SIDEKICK BECOMES SUPERHERO!
IF YOU LIKE CAPTAIN AWESOME, YOU'LL LOVE SUPER TURBO!

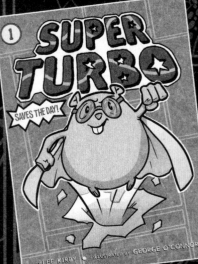